LIBERTY'S
CIVIL RIGHTS ROAD TRIP

MICHAEL W. WATERS

Illustrated by
NICOLE TADGELL

flyaway
books

Liberty woke up from a nap on the bus. "Are we there yet, Mom?"

"Not yet," said her mother. "We have a few hours left."

"Where is there again?" Liberty asked.

Her mom chuckled. "The first stop is Jackson, Mississippi."

"Is Jackson where we cross the bridge that you and Daddy told me about?"

"Not yet. Not until Selma."

"I can't wait," said Liberty. "I love bridges!"

Liberty turned and saw all the friendly people she'd met when they boarded the bus together in Dallas, Texas. Ms. Rachel, with her long locs, sat next to Mr. Adam. Ms. Alia sat in front of Dr. Glenn and near other new friends. The driver was Mr. Joe. Liberty's mom, dad, brother, and sister were on the bus, and so was her friend Abdullah and his family. Everyone was ready for their civil rights road trip.

Liberty was glad Abdullah was with her. She
always called him her cousin, even though they
weren't related. They sat together playing games
as hills, lakes, rivers, and trees passed by.

A long time later, Abdullah asked, "Mom, are we there yet?"

"We're here!" said his mom. "Welcome to Jackson, Mississippi."

The bus stopped at a small house, and everyone piled out. Liberty liked the house's aqua color, which reminded her of the ocean.

"Whose house is this?" she asked.

Ms. Rachel said, "Medgar Evers lived here a long time ago. He was a brave soldier in World War II, and he later worked for Black people to have the right to vote here in Mississippi."

"My mom and dad take me with them to vote!"
Liberty exclaimed.

"Mine too!" said Abdullah.

After everyone had visited the house and heard more
about Medgar Evers, the bus left for the next stop.

As the miles passed, Liberty saw how the land changed from dark brown to nearly red. "Are we almost there, Dad?" she asked. "Yes, Liberty, we're here!" said her dad. "Welcome to Glendora, Mississippi."

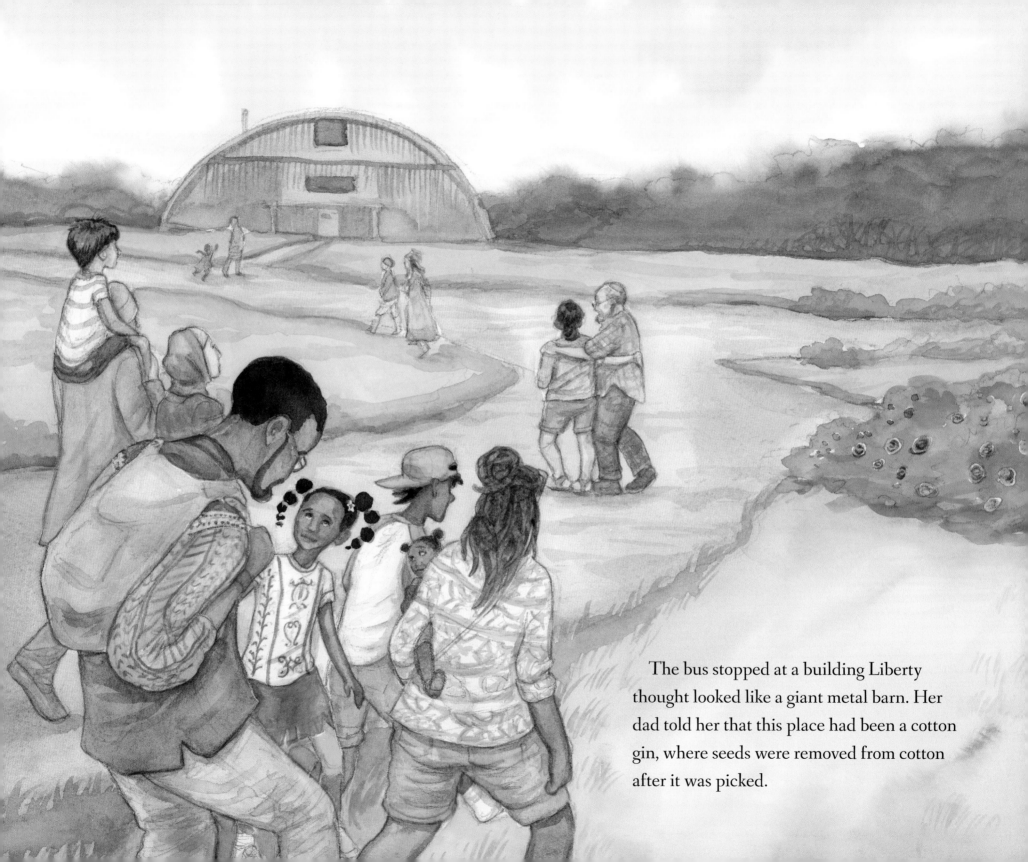

The bus stopped at a building Liberty thought looked like a giant metal barn. Her dad told her that this place had been a cotton gin, where seeds were removed from cotton after it was picked.

They were there to remember a boy named Emmett Till, whose death years ago had inspired many others to stand up for the rights of Black people. Liberty was surprised that Emmett hadn't been much older than her brother.

As everyone heard more about Emmett Till, Liberty and Abdullah curled up in their mothers' arms. It had been a long day.

The next morning, after a good night's rest, the
bus rolled on. Soon Mr. Joe announced from the
driver's seat, "We're here! Welcome to Memphis,
Tennessee."

As the bus stopped, Liberty saw a building with
many matching doors, each with a different number.
A large, round wreath hung near number 306.

As everyone looked quietly at door 306, Liberty's mom told her that this was the place where Dr. Martin Luther King Jr. had been killed. Liberty felt sad when she remembered that Dr. King had had children who were just like her, and then she thought about what Dr. King had done to help bring people together. Her dad had told her about Dr. King's dream for a better day, when everyone would be treated equally.

Liberty liked the sound of Dr. King's deep voice. She'd heard it on a recording of his "I Have a Dream" speech. As everyone looked around, she and Abdullah took turns trying to sound like Dr. King. They couldn't help laughing. Even though the Lorraine Motel was a serious place, Liberty imagined that Dr. King had liked to laugh, just like her dad did with her.

Hours later on the bus, Mr. Adam nudged Liberty and Abdullah awake. "We're here! Welcome to Birmingham, Alabama. We're at the Sixteenth Street Baptist Church."

As everyone left the bus, Liberty saw many stairs she could hardly wait to climb, across the street from a park full of trees.

"Can we go play?" asked Abdullah.

"Only after we pay our respects," said his mom.

As they walked in, Liberty heard someone say that four girls had died at the church when a bomb went off a long time ago. She did not like that at all.

"Who were those girls?" Liberty asked.

"They were friends who went to Sunday school together, and they sang in the children's choir," said Mr. Adam. "I'm sure they liked to have fun together. But some people did not like that Black people worshiped and fought for justice here."

"No one should be hurt in a church," Abdullah said.

"That's true, Abdullah," said his dad. "And no one should be hurt in a mosque, a temple, a synagogue, or anywhere."

Later, as everyone went outside, Abdullah shouted, "Come on, Liberty!" They ran across to the park and climbed trees until it was time for the bus to leave. Liberty wondered if the four girls had played there together before Sunday school.

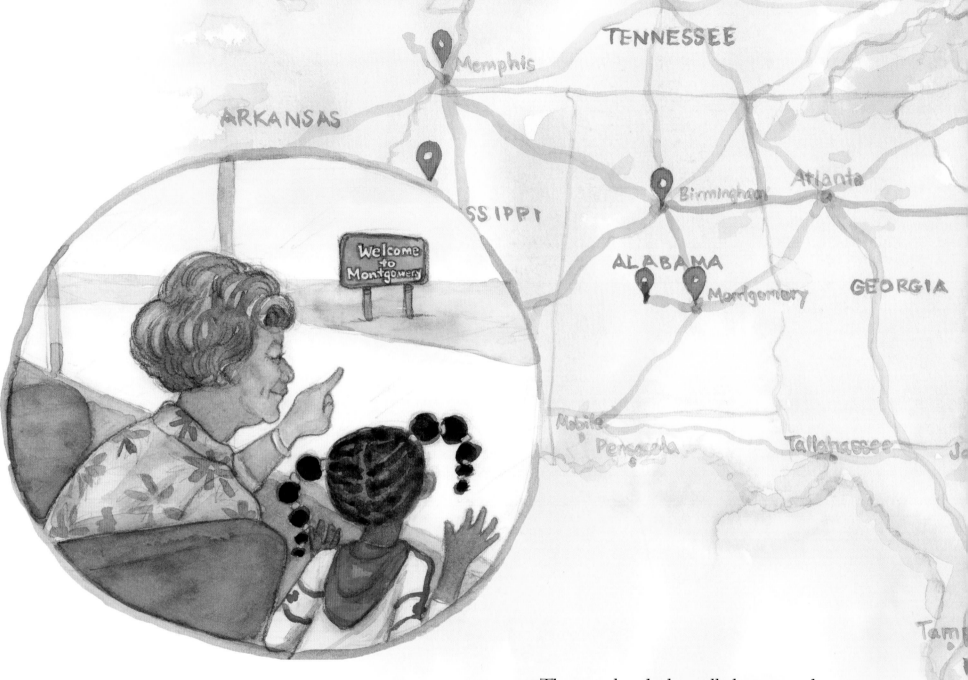

The next day, the bus rolled on to another
city. Ms. Alia turned to Liberty. "We're here!"
she said. "Welcome to Montgomery, Alabama."

"Whose house is this?" Liberty asked as everyone got off the bus in front of a small house with a large front porch.

"When Dr. King was the pastor at Dexter Avenue Baptist Church, this was his family's home," said Ms. Alia. "They had some happy times here, but the porch still has a hole in it left by a bomb. Thankfully, everyone was okay. Even in danger, Dr. King and his wife, Coretta, didn't let anything stop them from helping others."

Liberty and Abdullah knelt on the porch and put their hands into the hole.

How had Dr. King and his family been so brave? Liberty wondered.

The next day was the one Liberty had been waiting for. The bus rolled on and on. Finally she shouted, "I see it! There's the bridge!"

"Yes, we're here!" said Liberty's dad. "Welcome to Selma, Alabama."

The bus stopped near one end of the bridge. As everyone got off, Liberty said, "Tell me again why this bridge is important, Dad."

Her dad smiled. "A long time ago, brave women, men, and children crossed this bridge as they marched from Selma to Montgomery. They wanted to send a message that the laws of Alabama should be the same as those across America, which said that every citizen could vote. Some marchers were hurt by police officers who thought Black people shouldn't vote, but that didn't stop them. A few weeks later, they marched into Montgomery—fifty miles away! Black people can now vote in every state. This bridge is a symbol of everything people have faced to be seen as true Americans. It reminds us to be courageous as we work together to make our country better for all." Then he called out, "Let's march, everyone!"

Liberty and Abdullah grabbed the nearest hands as everyone began to cross together, just like the first marchers. As they walked, Liberty thought about all the places she had seen and the brave people she had heard about.

Then she turned and looked behind her, just as she did on that first day on the bus. So many people, all different, traveling together.

Liberty's dad looked around and said, "This is what America looks like." Liberty wasn't quite sure what that meant, but she liked how it sounded.

Liberty smiled at her dad and said, "Maybe this is what love looks like too!"

When the road trip had started, she had known only a few people on the bus. Now they were all part of her family. She didn't know where they would travel next. But she knew that wherever they went together, love would take them there.

A Note from the Author

The year 2020 brought the passing of two towering figures of the American civil rights movement of the 1960s: Congressman John Lewis, a courageous freedom fighter who helped lead the Bloody Sunday march in Selma in 1965, and the Reverend Dr. Cordy Tindell "C. T." Vivian, a key adviser of the Reverend Dr. Martin Luther King Jr. As time goes by, we continue to lose the foot soldiers of the movement. The preservation of their memories has never been more important.

My passion for connecting emerging generations with these foot soldiers inspired me to found the Southern Methodist University Civil Rights Pilgrimage nearly two decades ago. I continue to lead groups on pilgrimages through the Deep South, witnessing sites significant to the movement and inviting conversation with those who contributed to our freedom during those historic days of struggle.

To commemorate the fiftieth anniversary of the 1968 assassination of Dr. King, I led a civil rights pilgrimage for faith leaders from Dallas. Our bus was filled with a diverse group of many ages, including my wife and children and my dear friend Imam Dr. Omar Suleiman and his family. My daughter Liberty and her friend Abdullah Suleiman were the youngest on the journey.

Much of what is experienced along these pilgrimages is painful. Each day we travel to places where great brutalities were enacted and lives were often lost. Yet throughout this trip, Liberty and Abdullah turned these harrowing spaces into hopeful ones. Seeing these familiar places through their innocent and inquisitive eyes was a transformative experience that inspired me to write *Liberty's Civil Rights Road Trip*. It is my great hope that engaging history through the eyes of young friends will compel readers to learn more about the great contributions these American heroes have made to our nation and world.

During our stop in Atlanta, I had the opportunity to introduce Liberty to Dr. C. T. Vivian. I encouraged her to thank him, saying, "Without Dr. Vivian, your mommy, daddy, and even you one day would not be able to vote." This was striking to Liberty, who often comes with us to the polls. She walked up to Dr. Vivian, smiled widely, and said, "Thank you!" Dr. Vivian greeted her with just as wide a smile and said, "You're welcome!"

This heartfelt exchange is just a glimpse of what can happen if we talk about the stories and sacrifices of our history with our children. As these children grow up, may they continue to transform the brutal spaces in our world to places of peace, justice, and love. May we all join with them to do the same.

—MICHAEL W. WATERS

MORE ABOUT PLACES AND PEOPLE FROM LIBERTY'S TRAVELS

Liberty's journey offers an introduction to selected places and people that marked turning points in the American civil rights movement.

JACKSON, MISSISSIPPI—MEDGAR EVERS

Medgar Evers (1925–1963) is known for his activism in overturning segregation and expanding voting rights. Born in Decatur, Mississippi, he and his siblings would walk twelve miles a day to attend segregated schools. After serving in World War II and graduating from college, he became the first Field Secretary of the National Association for the Advancement of Colored People (NAACP) in Mississippi, a dangerous assignment. His assassination at his home on June 12, 1963, sparked protests in support of educational integration and voting rights. His house is now the Medgar and Myrlie Evers Home National Monument. nps.gov/memy

GLENDORA, MISSISSIPPI—EMMETT TILL

Emmett Till (1941–1955) was a fourteen-year-old boy from Chicago who was lynched during a visit with relatives in Mississippi. Accused of speaking to a white woman in a way that she found offensive, he was murdered by her family and others who were later acquitted, despite a subsequent confession and payment to print their story. A heavy metal fan from a cotton gin, where cotton was processed after picking, was used to weigh down Till's body in the Black Bayou, which spills into the Tallahatchie River. The brutality of the crime and the outcome of the trial drew national attention and outrage, helping to trigger significant events of the movement in the later 1950s and 1960s. The cotton gin building now houses the Emmett Till Historic Intrepid Center. glendorams.com

MEMPHIS, TENNESSEE—THE LORRAINE MOTEL—REV. DR. MARTIN LUTHER KING JR.

The Reverend Dr. Martin Luther King Jr. (1929–1968) was the most prominent leader in the civil rights movement. As an advocate for nonviolent resistance, he led such momentous demonstrations as the 1955 Montgomery bus boycott, delivered his famous "I Have a Dream" speech from the Lincoln Memorial during the 1963 March on Washington, and received the Nobel Peace Prize in 1964. On April 4, 1968, while staying at the Lorraine Motel during a trip to Memphis to support striking sanitation workers, Dr. King was assassinated outside Room 306. The Lorraine Motel is now part of the National Civil Rights Museum. civilrightsmuseum.org

BIRMINGHAM, ALABAMA—SIXTEENTH STREET BAPTIST CHURCH AND KELLY INGRAM PARK

Built in 1884, the Sixteenth Street Baptist Church became a gathering place for many notable Black people during the civil rights movement. On a Sunday morning, September 15, 1963, white supremacists planted a bomb that injured many people and killed four girls, aged eleven to fourteen: Addie Mae Collins, Cynthia Wesley, Carole Robertson, and Carol Denise McNair. The murder of children in a place of worship drew wide attention, and this event is thought to have helped drive passage of the Civil Rights Act of 1964. Across the street from the church is Kelly Ingram Park, where young protesters were sprayed with water from firehoses in 1963. It now features statues based on Birmingham's civil rights past, including one honoring the four girls. The church is a National Historic Landmark. 16thstreetbaptist.org

MONTGOMERY, ALABAMA—DEXTER AVENUE BAPTIST CHURCH PARSONAGE

The Reverend Dr. Martin Luther King Jr. was the pastor of Dexter Avenue Baptist Church from 1954 to 1960. The Montgomery bus boycott was planned in the church's basement. Dr. King lived in the church's parsonage with his wife, Coretta Scott King; two of their children, Yolanda and Martin III, were born during this time. The parsonage was bombed several times; the impact of one explosion can still be seen on the front porch. In 1960, the King family left Montgomery for Atlanta, Georgia, where Dr. King became copastor of Ebenezer Baptist Church and where their children Dexter and Bernice were born. The house in Montgomery is now the Dexter Parsonage Museum. dexterkingmemorial.org/tours

SELMA, ALABAMA—EDMUND PETTUS BRIDGE

To draw attention to the lack of voting rights for Black people, a peaceful march from Selma to Montgomery was planned for March 7, 1965. The march included crossing the Alabama River by way of the Edmund Pettus Bridge, where the unarmed demonstrators were met with violence from police. The graphic televised images of the confrontation awoke support for the twenty-year-old Selma Voting Rights Movement, and the event became known as Bloody Sunday. The bridge is now a National Historic Landmark, and commemorative marches across the bridge continue to honor the courageous marchers. civilrightstrail.com/attractions/edmund-pettus-bridge

For more locations and events that shaped the civil rights movement, follow the Civil Rights Trail. www.civilrightstrail.com

For my daughter Liberty.
Thank you for allowing me to see the world through your eyes.
It is an immensely beautiful place. I love you forever.
—M. W. W.

In memory of Samuel Walter Lee, my father and my first hero
—N. T.

Text © 2021 Michael W. Waters
Illustrations © 2021 Nicole Tadgell

First edition
Published by Flyaway Books
Louisville, Kentucky

21 22 23 24 25 26 27 28 29 30–10 9 8 7 6 5 4 3 2 1

Book design by Allison Taylor
Text set in Fanwood
Library of Congress Control Number: 2021009368
PRINTED IN CHINA

Most Flyaway Books are available at special quantity discounts when purchased in bulk by corporations, organizations, and special-interest groups. For more information, please e-mail SpecialSales@flyawaybooks.com.